C000233558

PICK ME, PICK ME POETRY

WRITTEN BY MARIA SMALLMAN

ILLUSTRATED BY ERICA WARBEY

ABOUT THIS BOOK

A collection of light-hearted,
humorous poetry for children.

This book is a work of fiction. Names, characters, places and incidents are the product of the author's imagination or are used fictitiously. Any resemblance to actual events, locales or persons living or dead is coincidental.

THIS BOOK IS DEDICATED TO …

To my three beautiful children, Oscar, Oliver and Sophia who have inspired many of the words in this book.

– Maria Smallman

Dedicated to Simon, Jessica-Rose and Leon; keeping life creative and fun.

– Erica Warbey

Table of Contents

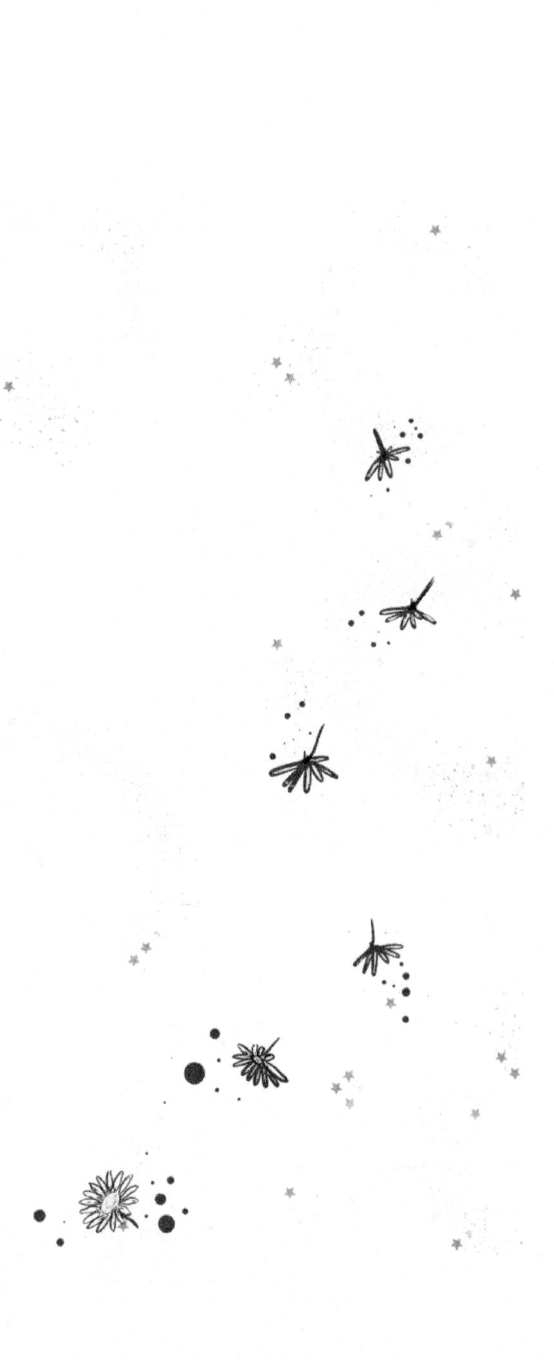

Rainbow gold

A sprinkle of rain, add bright rays of sun

Neither too hot nor too cold

Wait for the rainbow to spread through the sky

Then quick, let's go find the gold

SQUEAKY NIBBLER

There's a squeak in the cupboard

Where we keep all the snacks

And small, tiny holes

Chewed through chocolate wraps

There's a hole in the cupboard

A small hole in the base

If you sit and you wait

You might see a small face

It's a sweet, squeaky nibbler

With whiskers and tail

That gobbles up treats

On a monster-size scale

At least that's what I'm told

But I've not seen a trace

Just chocolate all over

My big brother's face

Wizard School

I've started lessons at wizard school,
I'm really learning quick

They gave me a wizard hat, a cloak
and a wizard stick

They asked which spells I had learnt,
which spells I now could do

"Can you turn your face from pink to
green then blue?"

"Yes, I can, watch this trick!"

I waved my magic wizard stick

"Ta da... My face from pink to
green then blue"

"That's very good, clever you!"

Can you magic ears so big

Sprout a tail, like a pig

Grow yourself 10 foot tall

Then shrink your feet super small?"

"Yes, I can, I can do that trick"

I waved my magic wizard stick

A face from pink to green then blue and ears so very big

I grew a curly tail, just like a little pig

I magicked myself 10 foot tall, then shrunk my feet super small

"Ta da... How's that? I magicked it all!"

"That's very good, clever you

Which magic tricks can you undo?"

"Oh," I say with slight regret...

"None, I haven't learnt that yet!"

Decisions, decisions

Gosh, I'd love the brownie, please
No, wait, I've changed my mind
I think I'll have the ice cream
Fudge and chocolate chip combined

No, actually, I'd rather
Take a sticky toffee pie
But then they have the waffles
Which I'd really love to try

Oh look, they have banoffee
Which I simply can't resist
I think just bring me everything
You have here on this list

Spider

Dingle, dangle by a thread

Weave a monster spider web

Catch a moth, trap a fly

Spin them up and mummify

Wait until you've rot and mush

Gooey bodies turned to slush

Spider's hungry, time to eat

Dinner's ready, what a treat!

THE OLDE SWEET SHOP

The olde worlde sweet shop
It's been there a hundred years
Wooded shelves, tubs and scales
And sweets that disappear

Butterscotch, flavoured drops
Liquorice and pears
Sherbet dip, soft midget
Fudge and gummy bears

If I ran that sweet shop

I'd gobble every treat in sight

The sweet shop of a hundred years

Would be out of business over night

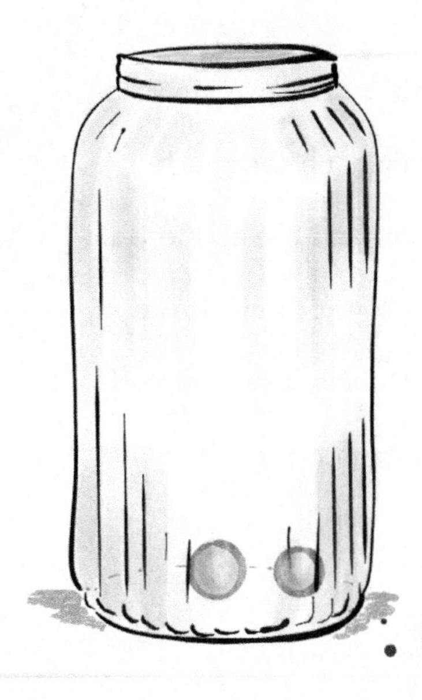

Shoelaces

These shoelaces come undone

I tie them up so tight

I tie them fifty times a day

But they never stay tied right

They get me in such trouble

"Tie your shoelaces," they say

Do they not know how many times

I've tied them up today?

These shoelaces are such a pain

I'm not sure what I should do

I think that I might cut them off

Else stick them down with glue

ALPHABET SMART

I gobbled up the alphabet

I thought it would make me smart

I gobbled every letter down

On the letter chart

Now I do not know the words

That come into my head

And no one seems to understand

A single word I've said

I might now have to swallow

A giant dictionary

To brush up on the words

In my vocabulary

Feed the Cat

My mum ran out this morning

Calling "Can you feed the cat?"

"Mum, what shall I feed him?"

"Some jam, he likes that"

I was a little puzzled

I'd never fed him that before

But before I could ask again

My mum was out the door

So I put the jam in the cat's bowl

A great blob for our little stray

And I thought no more about it

Until later on that day

My mum, she wasn't happy

Sticky paw prints everywhere

On the worktops, on the sofa

And the carpet up the stairs

She asked me what had happened

I said, "I've not a clue

I did exactly as you asked

And fed the cat for you."

"But what did you feed him

This doesn't look like ham"

"Well, no, I guess it wouldn't

Because I gave him jam"

CLEVER TRICKS

Do you have a clever trick

Like wriggling your ears

Can you roll your tongue

Or cry fake deliberate tears

Can you speak in funny voices

Or sing just like a bird

Do you have a riddled language

Speak in secret coded word

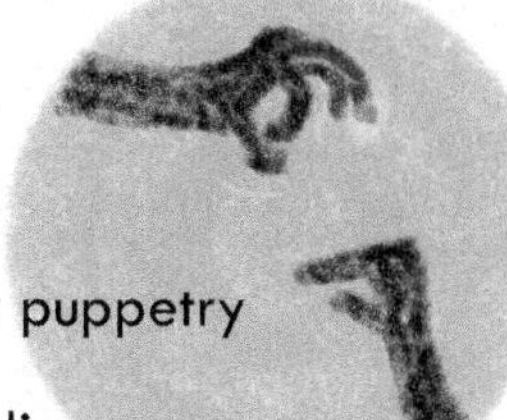

Can you shadow puppetry

Or make things disappear

Can you juggle beanbags

Pull things from behind your ear

Can you do the robot dance

Cartwheel or high kick

Do you have a funny talent

What is your clever trick?

TOOTH FAIRY

Have you ever seen the tooth fairy?

I think I did last night

I couldn't get to sleep

But had my eyes shut fairly tight

She must have thought that I was sleeping

As in the room she flittered

All twinkly and shiny

Shimmery and glittered

A bag upon her shoulder

To carry all milk teeth

She headed for my pillow

Where my tooth lay underneath

She must have then realised

That I was not asleep

As she sprinkled magic fairy dust

That sent me dreaming deep

And in the morning when I woke

I was not sure what I had seen

Did I see the tooth fairy,

Or was it all a dream?

Crocodile

Beware the hungry crocodile

He looks fake at a glance

He'll trick you with his clever freeze

His frozen wide-mouthed stance

You'll creep a little closer

He's made of wax for sure

But too close to Mr Crocodile

He'll snap you in his jaw

THE CLOCK IN THE HALLWAY

The clock in the hallway is awfully loud

It dings and it dongs in a chime

The hands they both spin around and around

If only I could tell the time

A LITTLE TOO LITTLE

Can you nearly do it

Are you almost nearly there

If you tippy tippy-toe

Or spike up all your hair

If you stand a little taller

Just an inch or two

If they're super-duper nice

They might still let you through

Shall we queue? Want to try it?

Shall we stand and wait in line?

Never mind, it doesn't matter

You'll be big enough next time

Fly high, what am I?

Gliding, soaring, flying high

A bird without its wing

Distracted momentarily

They let go of the string

The skies of blue changed suddenly

Now vast skies of grey

A super gust of blizzard wind

Carries me away

Full force I blow into a tree

Knot round a leafy limb

I pull, I tug but can't break free

Twigs ripping at my skin

The air now heavy, damp and cold

Get ready for the rain

Mangled, torn and tied in knots

I'm not sure I'll fly again

A WITCH NEXT DOOR

I'm fairly certain but can't be sure

The sweet little lady that lives next door

With big hooked nose and voice high pitch

Could she maybe be a witch?

She has a cat, that fits my theory

Her house is dark and damp and eerie

Her teeth all stained with crooked grin

And a rather large protruding chin

She seems so nice, but I'm still not sure

If we have a witch living next door

Wandering dinner

A sprout rolled off my plate

Followed by a pea

Then off leapt a carrot

And a slice of my turkey

It all fell off my plate

And dropped under the table

I would have eaten all of it

It's a shame I'm now not able

I'm very glad my pudding bowl

Doesn't spill in the same way

It's clever that the bowl has sides

To ensure it doesn't stray

Shoes for Best

These shoes they rub, these shoes they chafe

But don't they look so pretty

I think they're just a pinch too small

It's really such a pity

I kept them in a special box

My very favourite pair

On a shelf, in my room

Reserved for special wear

A wedding, party, dinner

I never put them on

My special shoes, just far too nice

But now the chance has gone

These shoes are now far too small

Pretty as they are

My lovely shoes, the time has come

To wish you au revoir

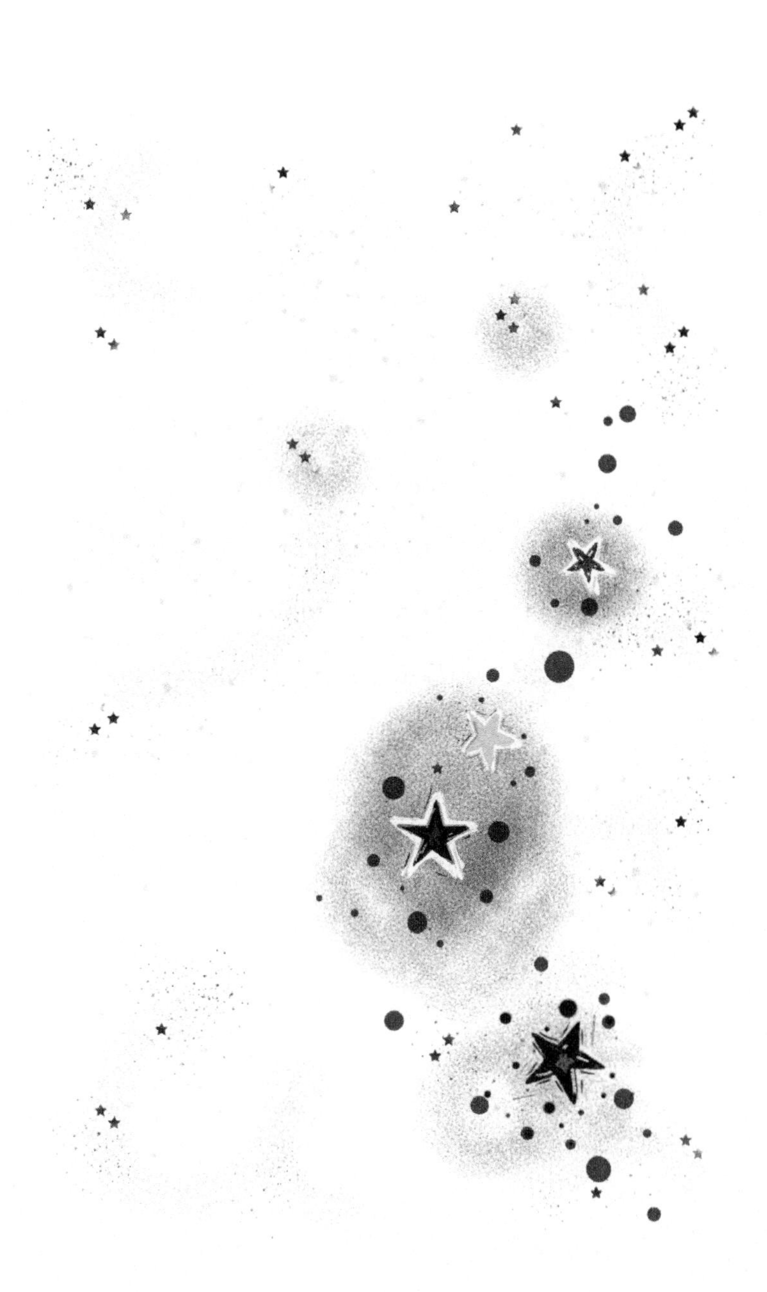

Dawdler

Don't dilly dally

Keep on moving, nearly there

Stop dawdling

Dragging your feet, I do despair

Move a little faster

Put some gusto in, let's go

I do not understand

How you move quite so slow!

Hide and seek

One, two, three

I'm waiting

Four, five, six

Are you done?

Seven, eight, nine

Are you ready?

I'll give you until ten

Here I come

Look how high

Look how high

Look how high

I kick my leg up

To the sky

Look how close

Look how near

My leg

It kicks up

To my ear

Look how I stretch

Look how I bend

Ouch...

That's not a move

I'd recommend

Camouflage Frog

He hides under a lily pad

Blends into all the green

His body a soft camouflage

To merge with every scene

Occasionally, you'll spy him

With a beady, hawk-like eye

Amongst the wet, leafy grass

You're master at I-Spy

You'll build a pool, a rockery

So he can swim in shade

You'll fill with things you think he'd like

You're pleased with what you've made

But where's he gone? You now don't know

He's nowhere to be seen

He's hiding in the underworld

Of pretty shades of green

Beach days

Long bright sunny days, days of
beach and sand

Sun hats, bucket, spade, ice cream in
your hand

Castle moats, sailing boats, rocks and
skimming stones

Shells up to your ear make different
sounds and tones

Rock pools, crabs and clams, fishing
nets and wait

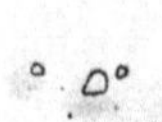

See what we can find with a bucket
full of bait

Beach balls, boogie boards, a walk along the shore

Flying kites in the breeze, let go and watch them soar

Sun lotion, wet towels, sand stuck to our skin

In the water, lukewarm, washed off with a swim

Long days, sun-bleached hair, golden skin all tanned

Sun cools, sun sets, shadows in the sand

Clever Cat

I overheard the cat today talking to the dog

I couldn't quite believe my ears; here goes the dialogue:

"Say Mr Dog, since you moved in, everything has soured

They used to stroke me lovingly, brush my fur for hours

They'd give me treats, play 'catch the string'

I was the boss, the catty king

But now you're here; you've stolen my throne

You've pushed me out of my own home

No cute meow, no gentle purr

Will sort these clumps of matted fur"

Cat silent now in her distress

Sat plotting how to fix this mess

Cat says to dog, "Come let me show you

This really clever trick I do"

The dog he follows, now intrigued

"We're going out without a lead"

The tiny patter of little paws

Cat walks dog through the double doors

Cat loses dog around the back

Then steps back in through the cat flap

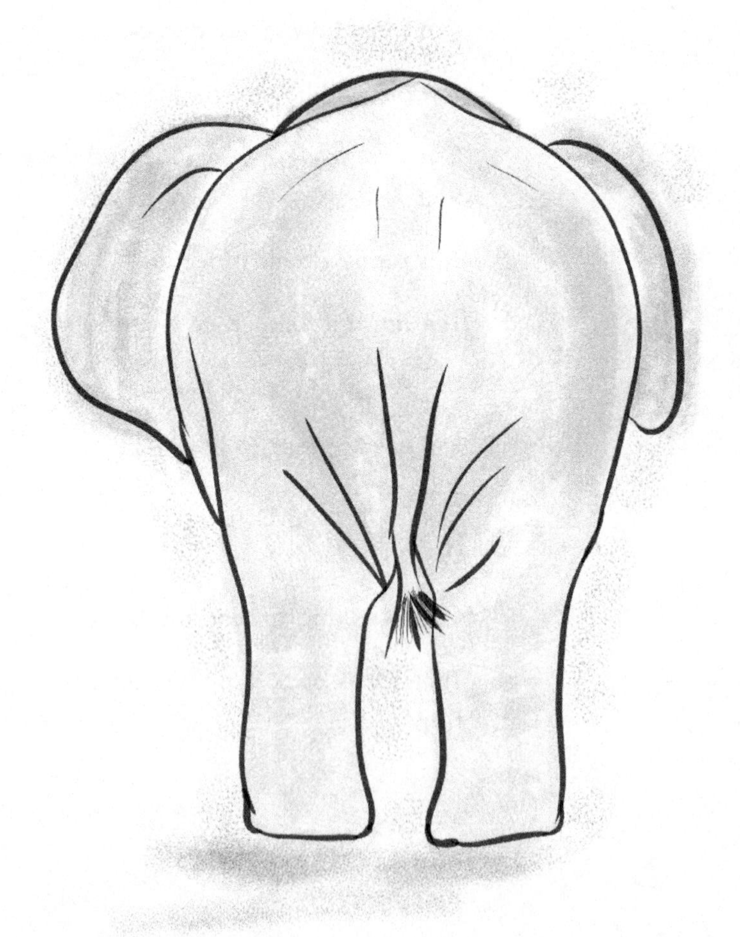

Forgetful Ellie

Ellie forgot where she came from a lot

So she wrote a note to remind her

But this didn't help not one little bit

As she forgot that she'd stuck it behind her!

The sink

The sink drank all the water

While I washed my hands

It must have been so thirsty

But I don't understand

It drank so much this morning

While I brushed and gave a rinse

And then again at lunchtime

And quite a few times since

How does it drink so much,

And where does it all go?

It puzzles me every time

I'd really like to know

THUNDERSTORM

It's wet, and it's windy

A dark, moody sky

A storm must be brewing

Soon thunder'll roll by

A flash lights the night

A roar load and fierce

The sky screaming out

With a deafening pierce

The smashes, the crashes

The bangs and the **boom**

Glad I'm tucked up in bed

All safe in my room

WHO MADE ALL THIS MESS?

Who's been in my room and made all this mess

Who's thrown all my things on the floor

Who's taken my books neatly stacked on the shelf

And emptied out my clothes drawer

Who unmade my bed, crumpled my sheets

Left dirty clothes in a pile

The plates in the corner, scattered in crumbs

They look like they've been here a while

Who tipped all their rubbish all over the place

I barely can get through my door

Ha … I am only joking

It looked just like this before!

My Granny's Bag

My Granny has a magic bag

That holds all you'd ever need

It's only very small

But supplies are guaranteed

Colouring books, felt tip pens

A bag of things to make

Tissues, cream and plasters

To patch a cut or scrape

She'll pack a book for reading

Two, sometimes three

And a little notebook

With a special pen for me

She keeps a puzzle book

The crossword all complete

And a small electric fan

In case I overheat

You'll find a mini board game

Seven games rolled into one

A sun hat and sun lotion

For sitting in the sun

She'll have a stash of biscuits

And lots of yummy treats

And if you dig deep enough

You'll find a bag of sweets

My Granny thinks of everything

And in her magic bag it goes

And just what we'll be needing

Only Granny knows

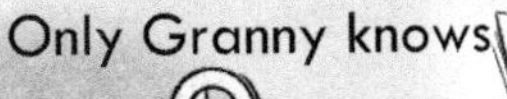

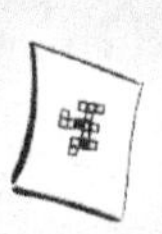

Holidays

A holiday, hip, hip hooray

My bags are packed; let's go!

I'm not sure where we're headed

If it's golden sand or snow

But I'm packed and I'm ready

Stood excited by the door

An adventure waiting for me

On another distant shore

I can't wait until we get there

I'm ready for some sun

Swimming in the warm pool

Sandy beaches here I come

We get there, all offload

Driven to our destination

But it looks like I'll be skiing

In a swimsuit with flotation

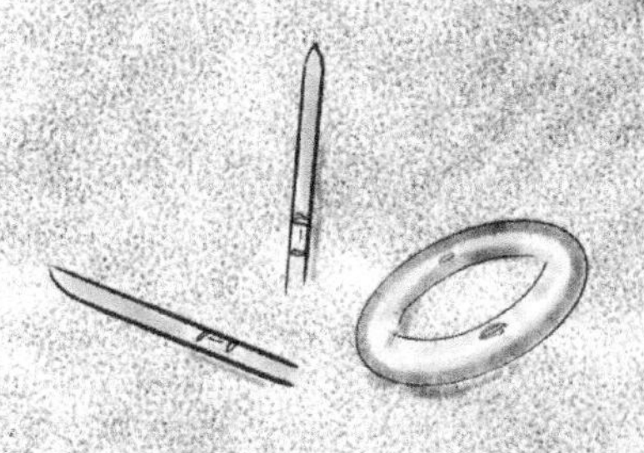

A small door

There's a small half-size door

Do I dare to go through

What's on the other side

On the count of three

Turn the handle gently

Let's open but not too wide

Feeling brave, take a peek

Can you see in the dark?

A dusty, damp space with no light

There are boxes on things

And things upon boxes

Crammed into a space small and tight

And the things in the boxes

All incredibly old

All worn with a musty old smell

Over time been forgotten

Collecting dust in the dark

But all with a story to tell

Walk Away, Walk Away

Walk away, walk away

Well, that's easy to say

But he's non-stop annoyed me all morning

I've told him to stop, told him "leave me alone"

He won't listen, so here comes my warning

"Do that again, I won't be so nice

I won't walk away or ignore

So try that again, if you're feeling brave

I dare you to try it once more"

The paving cracks

Be careful of the cracks,

The cracks you shouldn't tread

The cracks are oozing lava

A gooey burning red

Be careful of the cracks,

They'll swallow you down whole

They'll suck you down into

A dark and endless hole

Be careful of the cracks,

Be careful where you stand

The cracks are disappearing fast

It's super-sinking sand

Be careful of the cracks,

The cracks you shouldn't tread

Time to change the game up

Let's all walk backwards instead

Snail speed

Oh my, you move slow

Suckers stick, slide and go

It's a wonder you get anywhere at all

You spend the whole day slithering away

Not moved more than a brick up the wall

It's no bother, I guess

If you move more or less

But it must be frustrating for you

As you'll get to the top, one last push till you stop

But your stickers have run out of glue

And off you will slide

Like a whizz sort of ride

A speed I've not witnessed before

Back to square one, you've to start once again

Make your way slowly back up from the floor

The Cleaning Fairy

The cleaning fairy's been again; I never see her come

They tell me that she's pretty good and looks a bit like mum

Her jobs are fairly frequent, and there's not much respite

She works long hours most days, morning through to night

She cleans and dries the dishes and takes out every bin

Washes all our clothes, hangs them out then brings them in

She irons, and she folds, and she neatly puts away

She hoovers through the house almost every single day

She bleaches every toilet and wipes out every sink

If she didn't come to do all this, our house would really stink

The cleaning fairy does this; she does it all for free

When I know that most of the time, the mess was made by me

So thanks to the cleaning fairy for sorting all our mess

I'm glad you come to visit us and clean at this address

WELL DONE, DAD

Dad thinks he's good at certain things

"Manly things," he says

Like fixing the tumble drier

Or mending the chair leg

He insists that he can do it

"This won't take me long"

But you know once he's said that

It's fairly certain to go wrong

I could write a list of his disasters

The list would never end

We don't want to upset him

So instead, we all pretend

“Well done, Dad, good job there,

It’s working really well”

No one noticed it fall off again

Or that there’s a burning smell

We didn’t spot that it was backwards

That you missed out a few screws

It doesn’t lean too much

It looks great we all enthuse

Well done, our clever dad

You really get stuck in

Just a shame it’s now unusable

And it’s not long for the bin

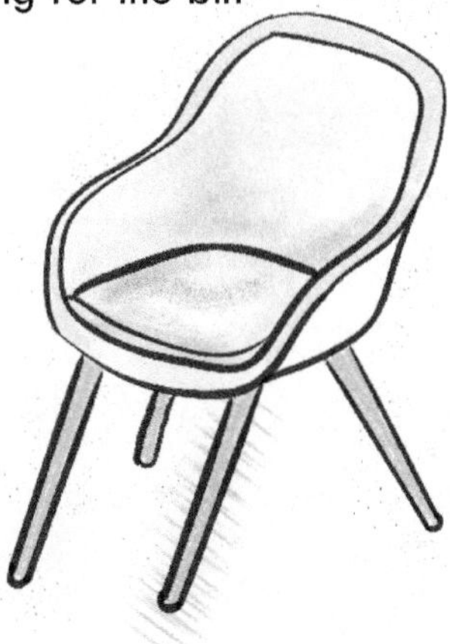

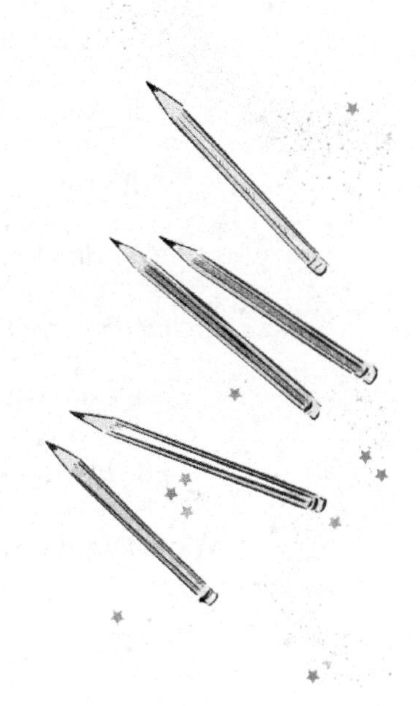

THE SORT OF DAY

It's the sort of day

That we'll all hide away

In dens with blankets and bears

It's the sort of cold

A hot chocolate to hold

Warms up all our insides

It's the sort of wet

You don't want to get

So we'll sit by the fire keeping warm

It's the sort of wild

For a wide-eyed child

Watching the start of a storm

Nothing to do

There's nothing to do, nothing to play

Mum has taken the iPad away

There's nothing to do; I'm fed up and bored

I'd set up the PlayStation but mum's unplugged the cord

There's nothing to do but sit here and moan

Mum's taken it all, the TV and phone

There's nothing to do, nothing to play

So I'll sit doing nothing for the whole of the day

Mum makes a suggestion that I should perhaps find

Something to engage my body and mind

Go build a den, go fly a kite

Go hang with friends, go ride your bike

Go read a book, go bake a cake

Go play with your toys or find something to make

Go make up stories, go make up games

Go play a sport, go fly paper planes

Go paint a picture, go do some drawing

You can't claim that it's all boring

So please go and find something to do

Or I will find some jobs for you

Stubborn tooth

This stubborn tooth, hanging by a thread

That refuses to pull from my gum

I've wibbled and wobbled, encouraged it out

In the hope the tooth fairy might come

I've prodded and poked, twisted and pulled

Jiggled, wiggled and nudged

But it seems set on staying, so loose in my mouth

As it simply cannot be budged

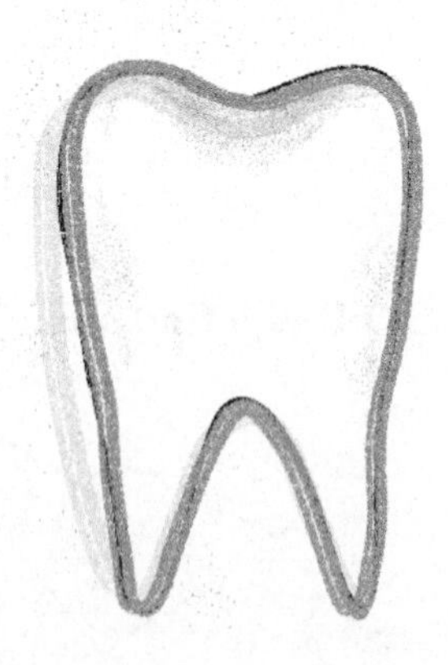

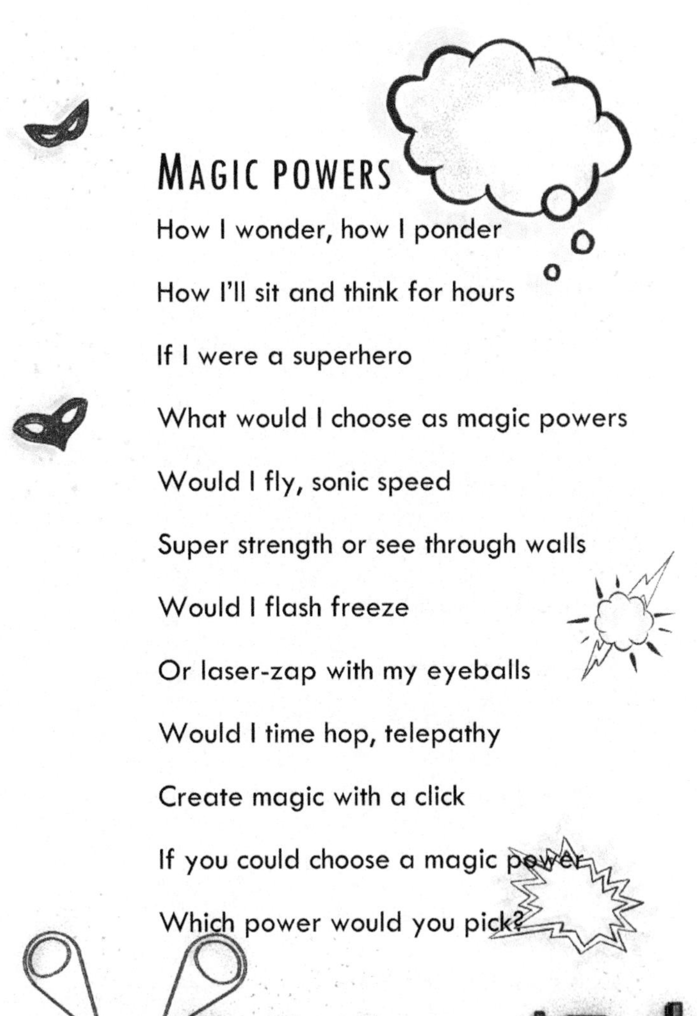

Magic powers

How I wonder, how I ponder

How I'll sit and think for hours

If I were a superhero

What would I choose as magic powers

Would I fly, sonic speed

Super strength or see through walls

Would I flash freeze

Or laser-zap with my eyeballs

Would I time hop, telepathy

Create magic with a click

If you could choose a magic power

Which power would you pick?

Bear dressed in Granny's clothes

The bear that stole our washing line
Is dressed in Granny's clothes
He looks a little funny
Dressed like Gran from head to toes

He has her little blouse on
And her cardie fits quite snug
The skirt's a little ruffled
And those tights need a good tug

Her shoes he's squeezed onto his feet
They look like they might split
But all in all, I have to say
It's not too bad a fit

Fairy Tree

There's a tree in the garden

A strange-looking tree

Its branches all hang to the ground

The roots are all twisted

They've all intertwined

To produce a mysterious mound

And the tree, so alive

You can feel the bark breathe

I'm sure that there's life from within

But I've looked, and I've looked

And I've checked every nook

I just can't find a way to get in

I wonder who lives

Who has burrowed beneath

In a world that can't quite be seen

I'd take a guess it's a fairyland

With a magical King and Queen

MAGIC PATH

Steppingstones, a magic path

Let's follow where it goes

Through some bushes, by a pond

Twigs snagging all our clothes

Up a hill, down a track

Thick tree roots to climb

Mossy hands, hideaways

The smell of sweet springtime

A broken wall, a golden key

A magic key for sure

A super search is underway

To find the magic door

THE HICCUPS

The hiccups, the hiccups, the hiccups

I have had them the whole of the morning

I've tried holding my breath, a drink upside down

Tried scaring, some counting and yawning

The hiccups, the hiccups, the hiccups

It doesn't look like I'll rid them too soon

I have counted beyond a thousand

And will hold the world record by this afternoon

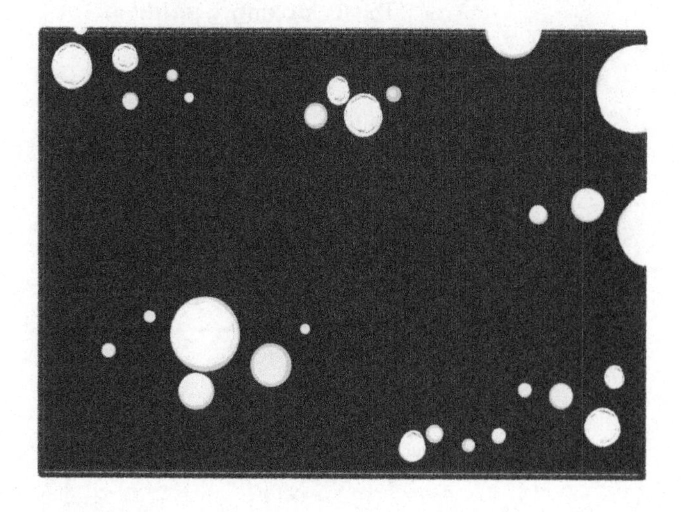

PAPER MACHE TEACHER

Gooey, sticky fingers

Newspaper torn to shreds

Pots of paint and tubs of glue

For paper mache heads

Mesh it all together

What can we create

A mini-masterpiece

This is looking great

I think it looks like teacher

But I really daren't say

As if our teacher knew

She'd keep us in at play

The circus

The circus is coming; it's coming to town

A huge pop-up tent, a big red-nosed clown

Candy floss, popcorn, toffee apples on sticks

Wonderous animals performing well-rehearsed tricks

Tightrope walkers and jugglers, strong man Hercules

Dancers on horses and men on trapeze

Magicians and magic, stunts crazy and wild

A memory to keep for every small child

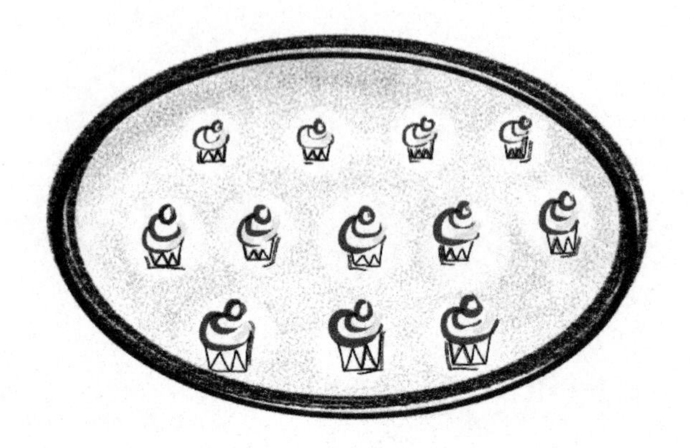

Piglet's Bakery

Pop into Piglet's Bakery

Iced buns, sponges and slices

Cheesecake, truffles and gingerbread

All baked with fruits and spices

Muffins, doughnuts, truffles

Meringue and sticky pies

All baked by Mr Piglet

To hungry piglet size

MAGIC SHOOTING STAR

A shooting star whizzed past last night

Shot across the darkened sky

Leaving small traces of magic dust

For all whom it passed by

I made a wish upon it

Watched it twinkle, watched it glow

And asked if it had heard my wish

That it could let me know

It shot so fast, a glitter trail

Spread in a super swish

It lit the sky so beautifully

It must have heard my wish

Index of titles

Acknowledgements

I have really enjoyed putting this book together and I hope there is something in here for every reader.

I'd like to thank my family for all their loving support and encouragement; especially my three children who have listened to most of these poems so many times they now know most by heart.

I'd like to thank Erica for all the beautiful illustrations and for so patiently working on the layout and format of the book, thank you!

I'd like to say a big thank you to all who have taken the time to read my book, I do hope you enjoyed it and a huge thank you to all that have bought my book.

Maria

Printed in Great Britain
by Amazon